"WHAT ABOUT ME?"

Said the Flea

**EDITED BY
IMOGEN CURRELL-WILLIAMS**

DESIGNED BY JACK CLUCAS

**COVER DESIGN BY
JOHN BIGWOOD**

First published in Great Britain in 2021 by Buster Books,
an imprint of Michael O'Mara Books Limited,
9 Lion Yard, Tremadoc Road, London SW4 7NQ

W www.mombooks.com/buster f Buster Books @BusterBooks

Text copyright © 2021 Lily Murray
Illustrations copyright © 2021 Richard Merritt
Layout and design © 2021 Buster Books

ISBN: 978-1-78055-701-4

2 4 6 8 10 9 7 5 3 1

This book was printed in December 2020 by Leo Paper Products Ltd,
Heshan Astros Printing Limited, Xuantan Temple Industrial Zone,
Gulao Town, Heshan City, Guangdong Province, China.

WRITTEN BY
LILY MURRAY

ILLUSTRATED BY
RICHARD MERRITT

FOR PETE – LM
FOR MAISIE AND MOLLY – RM

Sophia sits at her desk one day,

She picks up her pen ...

"Now what shall I say?"

She ponders and puzzles,
she **TWIRLS** her hair,

She munches an apple and **SWINGS** on her chair.

"I need to work out what my story's about ... "
When from the next page comes a **VERY**

LOUD
SHOUT!

"You should write about **ME**, I'm a unicorn,

I've got sparkly hooves and a glittery horn.

I'm magic ... I fly ...

I DO RAINBOW POO!"

"Ha!" comes a cry. "No one cares about you ... "

"You're just a horse with far too much hair,
All the best books have **AT LEAST ONE BEAR**."

"We make great picnics or, if you prefer,

You can snuggle up in our **SOFT, COSY FUR.**"

Sophia looks up ...

... Sophia looks down.

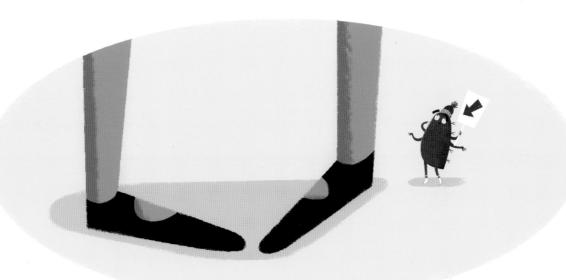

"What was that noise?" she asks with a frown.
"I'm sure I heard something. A sort of whine ..."

"Ignore it!" says Lion. "Aren't I *divine?*

Look at my mane! My shiny, gold crown!

I'm king of the jungle, talk of the town."

"I'm known for my style and my beautiful suits,

My marvellous robes and my high-heeled boots.

And not only that, I've got spotty pyjamas ... "

"Well, so do we!" LAUGH a couple of llamas.

"We've got **FLUFFY** coats
and funny long faces.

We love to pop up in *unusual places*.

Writing about us would be **SO EASY...** "

"The trouble is you're **way** too **CHEESY!**
Go for a sloth, I've much more charm,
I can hang from a branch by just one arm."

"But all you do is slumber and snooze ...
What about ME? I'm the one you should choose!"

Sophia looks left. Sophia looks right.

She looks out the window. There's nothing in sight.

"That noise," she wonders,
"Those high-pitched squeaks ... "
Then in **BURST** ten penguins,
snapping their beaks.

"Clearly **WE** are the stars of your show,

We're the most fun you can have in the snow.

We swim, we glide, we have flappety feet,

And we're really good at

HIDE-AND-SEEK!"

"But I'm never in stories," pleads the flea.

"Can't it be my turn? What about ME?"

Sophia starts searching all around,

"What on earth is that funny sound?"

Then, all at once, the page starts shaking.

"What's going on?" Sophia asks, quaking.

Enormous feet go STOMP! STOMP! STOMP!

Mighty jaws go CHOMP! CHOMP! CHOMP!

Next there comes a TERRIBLE ROAR!

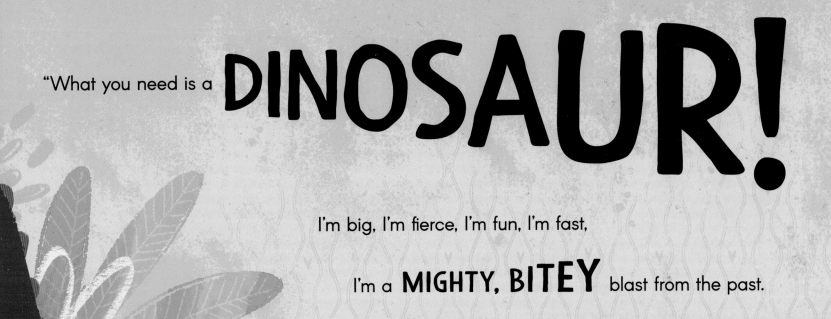

"What you need is a DINOSAUR!

I'm big, I'm fierce, I'm fun, I'm fast,

I'm a **MIGHTY, BITEY** blast from the past.

And, if you like, I can ask **ALL** my friends,

Wouldn't that make a wonderful end?"

"*Help!*" says the unicorn. "**NO!**" say the bears.

The terrified llamas hide under the chairs.

All ten penguins dive into a drawer.

Sloth clings to Lion, who runs out the door.

"STOP!" shouts Sophia. "Enough of this riot.
It's time to decide. Can you all please be quiet?"
She turns the first page but then

SOMETHING
GOES...

"Oh no," gulps Sophia.

"What was that?"

"It's me," sobs the flea. "I wished and I wished, Hoping you'd listen ... but now I'm all SQUISHED!"

"What were you trying to say,

LITTLE FLEA?"

"That maybe, just maybe,
you could write about ME?

I know that I'm small
and I haven't got style,
I can't do magic or give a
DAZZLING smile.

But I try to be **BRAVE** and I try to be **BOLD**,
Doesn't my story deserve to be told?"

Sophia sits at her desk one day.

She picks up her pen.

She knows **JUST** what to say ...

"What About Me?"
The Story of a Flea